Birthday Boy

For my birthday boys, Dan and Will – DT

First published 2007
Evans Brothers Limited
2A Portman Mansions
Chiltern Street
London W1U 6NR

British Library Cataloguing in Publication Data

Taylor, Dereen
Birthday boy. - (Twisters)
1. Children's stories
I. Title
823.9'2[J]

ISBN: 978 0237 53470 7 (hb)
ISBN: 978 0237 53469 1 (pb)

Printed in China

Series Editor: Nick Turpin
Design: Robert Walster
Production: Jenny Mulvanny

TWISTERS

Birthday Boy

Dereen Taylor
and Ruth Rivers

Evans

Pleased you came,

Two the same!

Sausages on sticks,

Party tricks.

Hide-and-seek,

Take a peek.

Is it a toy?

Go fetch, boy!

Time for tea,

Save some for me!

Sing and shout,

Blow them out.

A birthday do,

Because Patch is two!

Why not try reading another Twisters book?

Not-so-silly Sausage by Stella Gurney and Liz Million 978 0237 52875 1

Nick's Birthday by Jane Oliver and Silvia Raga 978 0237 52896 6

Out Went Sam by Nick Turpin and Barbara Nascimbeni 978 0237 52894 2

Yummy Scrummy by Paul Harrison and Belinda Worsley 978 0237 52876 8

Squelch! by Kay Woodward and Stefania Colnaghi 978 0237 52895 9

Sally Sails the Seas by Stella Gurney and Belinda Worsely 978 0237 52893 5

Billy on the Ball by Paul Harrison and Silvia Raga 978 0237 52926 0

Countdown by Kay Woodward and Ofra Amit 978 0237 52927 7

One Wet Welly by Gill Matthews and Belinda Worsley 978 0237 52928 4

Sand Dragon by Su Swallow and Silvia Raga 978 0237 52929 1

Cave-baby and the Mammoth by Vivian French and Lisa Williams 978 0237 52931 4

Albert Liked Ladders by Su Swallow and Tim Archbold 978 0237 52930 7

Molly is New by Nick Turpin and Silvia Raga 978 0237 53067 9

A Head Full of Stories by Su Swallow and Tim Archbold 978 0237 53069 3

Elephant Rides Again by Paul Harrison and Liz Million 978 0237 53073 0

Bird Watch by Su Swallow and Simona Dimitri 978 0237 53071 6

Pip Likes Snow by Lynne Rickards and Belinda Worsely 978 0237 53075 4

How to Build a House by Nick Turpin and Barbara Nascimbeni 978 0237 53065 5

Hattie the Dancing Hippo by Jillian Powell and Emma Dodson 978 0237 53335 9

Mary Had a Dinosaur by Eileen Browne and Ruth Rivers 978 0237 53337 3

When I Was a Baby by Madeline Goodey and Amy Brown 978 0237 53334 2

Will's Boomerang by Stella Gurney and Stefania Colnaghi 978 0237 53336 6

Birthday Boy by Dereen Taylor and Ruth Rivers 978 0237 53469 1

Mr Bickle and the Ghost by Stella Gurney and Silvia Raga 978 0237 53465 3

Noisy Books by Paul Harrison and Fabiano Fiorin 978 0237 53467 7

Undersea Adventure by Paul Harrison and Barbara Nascimbeni 978 0237 53463 9